PRESENTING

Little White Duck

FEATURING

The Narrator   Little White Duck   Little Green Frog   Little Black Bug   Little Red Snake

   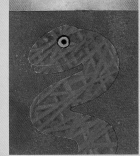

Lyrics by   Music by   Illustrations by

Walt Whippo   **Bernard Zaritzky**   **Joan Paley**

Little, Brown and Company
Boston   New York   London

Lyrics by Walt Whippo
Music by Bernard Zaritzky
Copyright © 1950 by COLGEMS-EMI MUSIC INC.
International copyright secured. All rights reserved. Used by permission.

Illustrations copyright © 2000 by Joan Paley

First Edition

Library of Congress Cataloging-in-Publication Data
Whippo, Walt.
  Little white duck / lyrics by Walt Whippo ; music by Bernard Zaritzky ; illustrations by Joan Paley. — 1st ed.
    p.   cm.
  SUMMARY: Based on the song of the same title, a little white duck causes a commotion in its pond.
  ISBN 0-316-03227-1
  1. Children's songs — United States — Texts. [1. Ducks — songs and music. 2. Songs.] I. Zaritzky, Bernard. II. Paley, Joan, ill. III. Title.
  PZ8.3.W57673 Li 2000
  782.42164'0268 — dc21   99-13661

10 9 8 7 6 5 4 3 2 1

TWP

Printed in Singapore

The collages in this book are a combination of cut paper, watercolor, crayon, and pastel. Watercolor washes along with crayon and pastel line were applied to textured and/or colored papers, which were then cut and layered to create a three-dimensional effect.

The text was set in Highlander. The display type was handlettered by the illustrator.

For Nicholas,
whose sense of composition and color in photography shines. Let this gift allow you to explore ideas and take you to wondrous places.

With love,
J.P.

Little White Duck

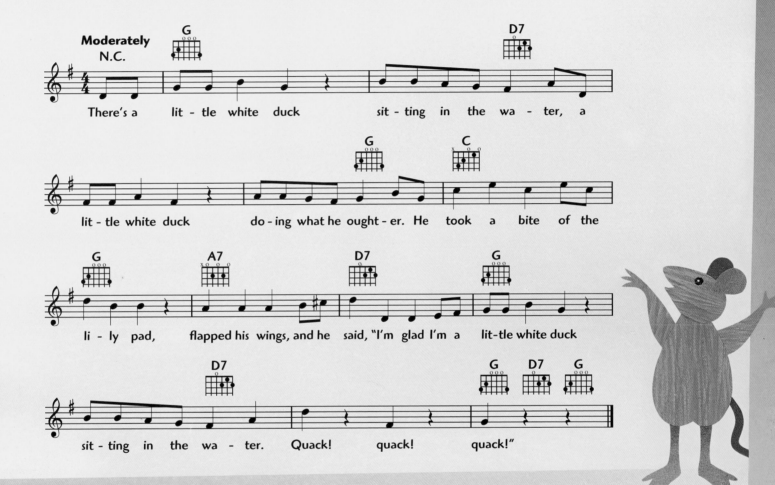

Lyrics by **Walt Whippo**   Music by **Bernard Zaritzky**

There's a little white duck sitting in the water,
A little white duck doing what he oughter.

He took a bite of the lily pad,
Flapped his wings, and he said, "I'm glad

I'm a little white duck sitting in the water."

QUACK!
QUACK!
QUACK!

There's a little green frog swimming in the water,
A little green frog doing what she oughter.

She jumped right off of the lily pad
That the little duck bit, and she said, "I'm glad

There's a little black bug floating on the water,
A little black bug doing what he oughter.

He tickled the frog on the lily pad
That the little duck bit, and he said, "I'm glad

There's a little red snake playing in the water,
A little red snake doing what he oughter.

He frightened the duck and the frog so bad,
He ate the bug, and he said, "I'm glad

Now there's nobody left sitting in the water,
Nobody left doing what they oughter.

There's nothing left but the lily pad.
The duck and the frog ran away—I'm sad

'Cause there's nobody left sitting in the water.